Jammin'~to~the~Sun

A Tribute to the Red Buses of Glacier National Park

PHOTOGRAPHY BY   BRET BOUDA

© 2010 Digital Broadway Publishing LLC
A Private Publisher

Jammin'-to-the-Sun is not meant to be read as you would read most books. Each image stands alone on an otherwise empty page and each is an attribute to the Glacier National Park "Reds" and their drivers of many generations responsible for visitors' memorable trips in one of the most beautiful national parks in our country.

A special thank-you to my family and friends for their support and encouragement in the process of doing it. I also want to acknowledge Tom Esch and Dave Eglsaer for their friendship, and for providing most of the captions and contributing to its accuracy, and to Michele Glaze for taking some of her precious time and finalizing our text in a professional manner. Acknowledgments to Matt Mullen for permission to reprint photographs of the Red Buses' rehabilitation process.

First Edition

Copyright 2010, Bret Bouda, all rights reserved.

A Digital Broadway Publishing LLC book

www.digitalbroadwaypublishing.com

ECO-FRIENDLY BOOKS
Made in the USA

ISBN # 978-1-61539-884-3

Printed in USA

The Red Buses of Glacier National Park

Glacier National Park as encountered today is the result of billions of years of change. From the Big Bang to last week's windstorm, agents of change have shaped this unique place. The depositing of layers of ocean sediment, the thrusting and twisting and uplifting of rock, the sculpting of the glaciers, and the relatively recent invasion of life forms such as trees and animals have all contributed to this perfect convergence of nature.

Then came mankind. Western mankind. Mankind that felt compelled to resolve the tension between the awe of nature and the need to see, control, exploit, and be safe in an environment as spectacular as Glacier.

How are we going to get people up that road? They need to be safe and comfortable. They need to be able to see out, smell the trees, and feel the spray of the waterfall. They need to do it in style. This is their vacation. We need to allow them to create memories of a lifetime."

In the 1930s the answer was the Red Buses. The architectural and engineering strife between functional form and the ornate is present in the Red Buses. They are functional. They can carry 17 passengers, and have five doors, big windows, comfortable seats, a retractable top, a fender step and handle, dual rear tires, and the infamous transmission and drive train that gave them the nickname *"**Jammers**".*

Yet the Red Buses are also ornate. Conceived during a time when art deco was a cultural movement, the buses project the elegance, glamour, and strength of an era that valued the perceived modern image. Look at the lines. Contrast the streamline curves of the bumper and fenders with the straight lines and repetition found in the grill. The grill lines are even repeated in the raised vertical front of the fender. Notice how both the grill and the windshield are wider at the top than at the bottom, a projection of power. The buses are a balanced collage of shiny steel, lacquer, and wood. The Red Buses are mobile art.

There is one artistic attribute that overwhelms all others. That is the use of the color red - Mountain Ash Berry Red to be exact, the same shade as the ripe mountain ash berries found in Glacier and shipped to Cleveland for matching. Not all White Motor Company buses of the 1930s were red. The color red is directly across the art color wheel from green. That is why red and green go together so well at Christmas. The red buses complement the green colors found in the fir, spruce, and larch of the mountain slopes. This red/green combination can also be found in the polished argillite stones of McDonald Creek. Red is the color of warmth. From the sunrise on Fusillade Mountain over St. Mary Lake to a Highline sunset over Heavens Peak, the color red is warmly found in the Park. Think Two Medicine or the view from Swiftcurrent Pass. Red can also be the color of extreme heat, as anyone who experienced the fire cresting Howe Ridge can attest.

In *Jammin'-to-the-Sun*, photographer Bret Bouda has captured the glamour of the Red Buses against the backdrop of the grandeur of the park. Bouda's other works, *Glacier Classics, Glacier Park Wide*, and his multipark work *The Magnificent Seven*, share the natural park experience. In this book Bouda celebrates the encounter of the mechanical with the natural, with the same purpose of the buses themselves, to enhance the experience of the park visitor.

It is hoped that Jammin' will honor the memory of the White Motor Company and bus designer Alexis de Sakhnoffsky, the Ford Motor Company that graciously restored and enhanced the buses, the careful stewardship of the National Park Service with its partner Glacier Park Inc., and the legions of drivers that for over seven decades have safely driven, educated, and entertained their guests. But the book's true purpose is the preser-

"Jammers" 1936 - 1939
back on the job

Bruce Gordon
*director of Ford's alternative fuel vehicles
said:*

*"Restoring the Red Buses has been
a bigger challenge than any of us
imagined, but it has also been a
labor of love to those involved.
We worked diligently to maintain
the historic integrity of the buses
and applied Ford's and TDM's
expertise in alternative fuel
vehicles and safety."*

Glacier's fleet of 33 red-with-black-trim vehicles was built
by White between 1936 and 1938. Glacier's Whites are
considered to be the oldest fleet of passenger-carrying
vehicles anywhere. Each one probably traveled about
600,000 miles over Glacier's roads before they were with-
drawn from service temporarily in 1999 for safety reasons.

Ford undertook an 18-month restoration of the buses in
2000 as a participant in the Proud Partner of America's
National Parks program, a partnership between Ford, the
National Park Foundation, the Glacier National Park
Service, and concessionaire Glacier Park Inc., which oper-
ates the park's bus fleet. TDM of Livonia, Michigan, was
contracted to work with Ford engineers and perform the
restoration.

"There is no more representative symbol of Glacier National Park than these classic Red Buses,"

said Jim Maddy, president of the National Park Foundation, as he witnessed the first of the striking red tour buses returning to Montana's Glacier National Park in June of 2002.

The vehicles now run on clean-burning LPG (propane) and are 93 percent cleaner than the original buses were when they were introduced in the park back in the 1930s.

The 17-passenger White touring sedans are more than a mere means of transportation for local residents and visitors — they are cherished, elegant symbols of the park's history. With their multiple doors and roll-back canvas tops, the Whites are as much a part of Glacier National Park as the Going-to-the-Sun Road on which they carry tourists across the Continental Divide.

Key Changes:

Powertrain/Fuel System - The original carbureted gasoline engine was replaced with a new fuel-injected 5.4L bi-fuel engine, capable of running on either gasoline or LPG (propane). An all-new exhaust system also was provided.

Chassis – The original chassis was removed and replaced with an E-450 chassis modified to fit the Red Bus body.

Brakes – The brake system was replaced with a production 4-wheel disc ABS system.

Windows and Lights – All windows were replaced with safety glass, and external lights were replaced or repaired and brought up to current standards. Along with the new technology, extreme care was taken to maintain the charm and historic integrity of the buses. Technology and safety were key elements, but comfort also was important.

Body – The original body of the Red Bus was carefully removed from the chassis. Damaged areas were repaired, cleaned, and repainted in the original color scheme. New sheet-metal or fiberglass components were blended into the vehicle where needed, such as in the fender wells and the rear door. In addition, all the door latches were replaced and composite aluminum sheeting took the place of the old plywood floors.

Seating – All passenger and driver seats were refurbished with new comfortable fire-retardant material. New padding was added to the handrails on the seat backs.

Running Boards – Running boards were replaced but remain consistent with the original design.

Ornamentation – When possible, original ornamentation was refurbished. When replacement was needed, it was done with component designs consistent with the original.

The famous Wild Goose Island is one of the most photographed spots by visitors to Glacier National Park.

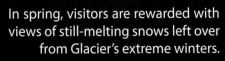

In spring, visitors are rewarded with
views of still-melting snows left over
from Glacier's extreme winters.

The previous generation of Glacier's touring vehicles, which operated during the 1920s.

On right, in the red shirt, Leroy Lott (1949–1950 Gearjammer)

Secret Valley Tour

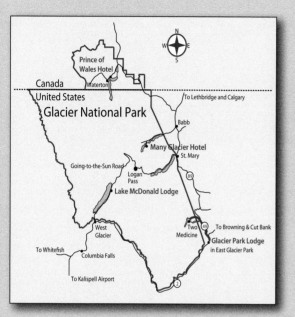

This tour goes off the beaten track in a valley that most who visit Glacier National Park do not even know exists.

Your tour starts at Glacier Park Lodge. Wind through the parklands along Two Medicine River, past Lower Two Medicine Lake to Middle Two Medicine Lake. While waiting for a ride on the historic wooden boat *Sinopah*, admire the towering peaks that surround you and visit the venerable Two Medicine Campstore, a landmark building and one of only three remaining log buildings built by the Great Northern *Railway* in Glacier National Park.

Later follow the flower-bedecked Pitamakan, a handicapped-accessible nature walk to Running Eagle Falls. Follow the 10,000-year-old Old North Trail back to Glacier Park Lodge, seeing the famous Lewis Overthrust along the way.

NOTE:
When the boat tour is unavailable, participants will receive a detailed Red Bus replica.

Entering the secluded Swiftcurrent Valley, which leads to Glacier's grandest lodge, the Many Glacier Hotel.

To many visitors, the bus itself is the centerpiece of any photo; the majestic mountains are merely the background.

Big Sky Circle Tour

The most inclusive tour of Glacier National Park starts with a morning drive over Marias Pass, which includes wildlife viewing at Goat Lick and a stop at the historic Isaac Walton Inn, a Mecca for railroad buffs.

After an optional lunch at Lake McDonald Lodge, tour the great cedar-and-hemlock forests around Glacier's largest lake. Then it is upward-bound to the alpine sections of the famous Going-to-the-Sun Road to Logan Pass and the backbone of the continent. Continue your drive through the St. Mary Valley with stops for viewing glaciers and Wild Goose Island Overlook. Your tour concludes with grand vistas of parklands, prairie, and peaks as you arrive back at your lodge.

The awe-inspiring alpine scenery of the Going-to-the-Sun Road is what brings visitors back year after year. Its glaciers are now gone, but Heavens Peak (on right) and its permanent snow dominate the view from much of the road.

29

At times along Going-to-the-Sun Road, pictures just can't capture the beautiful surroundings. Visitors are forced to step back, take a deep breath, and try to take it all in.

As John Muir stated, "Give a month at least to this precious reserve. The time will not be taken from the sum of your life. Instead of shortening, it will definitely lengthen it and make you truly immortal…."

The Jammers are always ready to offer assistance and answer questions.

Old North Trail Tour

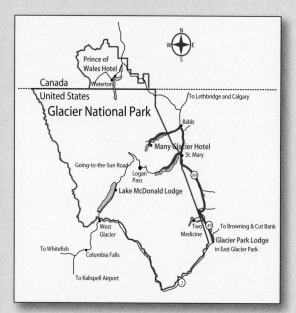

Follow the Old North Trail, a route used by Native people some 10,000 years ago, and visit three of Glacier's most beautiful valleys.

First, the Two Medicine Valley and a stroll to Red Eagle Falls along with a visit to the historic Two Medicine Campstore, then on to the Swiftcurrent Valley, one of the most beautiful valleys in the park. View three glaciers while having lunch at the incredible Many Glacier Hotel on the shore of Swiftcurrent Lake.

This valley is great for viewing an occasional bear. After lunch connect up with Going-to-the-Sun Road in the St. Mary Valley viewing the famous Wild Goose Island overlook.

Journey back to Glacier Park Lodge with incredible views of Montana's peaks and prairies wherever you look.

The "Line-Up" in front of the historic Lake McDonald Lodge.

Going-to-the-Sun Road is currently undergoing restoration by the National Park Service (NPS) and Federal Highway Administration (FHWA) to repair damages from the many avalanches and rock slides it sustained over the years. Repairs include fixing retaining walls, replacing the existing pavement with reinforced concrete, and working on tunnels and arches.

The buses' unique canvas tops offer guests a one-of-a-kind viewing experience of Glacier National Park. These tops, which can be easily opened and closed by the Jammers, offer excellent viewing and protection from the elements, when needed. In the heat of summer, however, with Glacier's bountiful sunshine, the Jammers will often roll back the tops before the tour even starts.

Eastern Alpine Tour

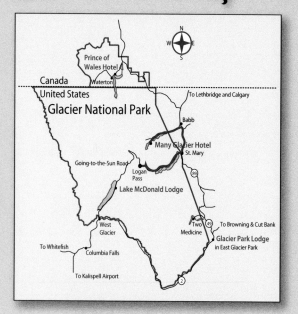

Start your tour on the unique and rugged East Front of the Rockies where geology flows from peaks to plains.

Then it is on to Going-to-the-Sun Road in the St. Mary Valley, where lakes, forests, and glaciers abound, until finally you are at the top of Logan Pass and the Crown Jewel of the Rockies. Blackfeet Indians called this place the backbone of the world. Continue back to your starting point amidst mountains live with wildflowers and water- falls that look different than they did just a few hours ago.

Western Alpine Tour

Start your tour in the great cedar-and-hemlock forests that lie within the Lake McDonald Valley. Travel up the famed Going-to-the-Sun road along glacier-carved arêtes, where views are breathtaking, waterfalls can cascade over the road, and wildflowers are everywhere! Your destination is the top of the Continental Divide at Logan Pass at a place described by old timers as the Crown of the Continent and the backbone of the world.

Although the Red Buses are no longer the only means to get around Glacier, they are the only vehicles to make stops for pictures and wildlife. In addition, the informative commentary of the drivers offers guests a great way to learn more about this beautiful park. Whether it's about the flora, the fauna, the geology, or the rich and storied history of the park and the Native Americans, visitors are sure to hear something that truly interests them.

The postcard-friendly Weeping Wall
along the Going-to-the-Sun Road.

Crown of the Continent Tour

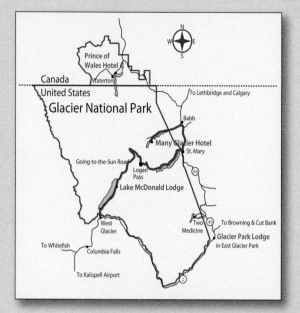

Starting from both the East and West sides of Glacier National Park, the Crown of the Continent Tour is one of the most popular tours in the park. The tour begins at the base of these majestic mountains and winds its way up to the Continental Divide at Logan Pass. From there experience breathtaking views in all directions before heading down to either Lake McDonald Lodge or the Many Glacier Hotel for an optional Lunch in one of the grand hotels of Glacier.

After lunch, head back over Going-to-the-Sun Road for a second chance to take in all the beauty and majesty that is, Glacier National Park.

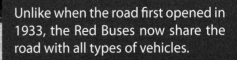

Unlike when the road first opened in 1933, the Red Buses now share the road with all types of vehicles.

The often-crowded Logan Pass is located at the highest point of the Going-to-the-Sun Road, 6,646 feet above sea level. Luckily, the Red Buses have reserved parking, so our guests can enjoy the 360-degree beauty of the Continental Divide.

Jammers, the drivers of the historic Red Buses, often use the buses' unique open tops to point out the many scenic features of Glacier National Park. The open top affords guests the opportunity to stand up at pullouts and enjoy picturesque mountains while remaining within the safety of the bus — especially expedient when in the presence of Glacier's most famous inhabitant, the grizzly bear.

Mountain Majesty Tour

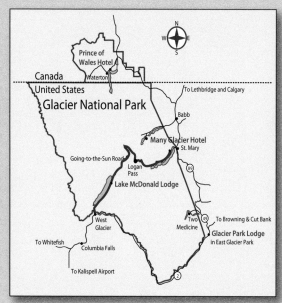

This famous "West Side" tour combines detailed exploration of two valleys with some of the best scenery in the world thrown in for good measure.

Start in the McDonald Valley, where forests of giant cedars, hemlock, and tamarack tower above the road and define the shores of Glacier's largest lake. Then it is up the Going-to-the-Sun Road, hanging on the side of the Garden Wall, the most beautiful arête in park, all the way up to the top of the Continental Divide at Logan Pass.

Learn the secrets of Going-to-the-Sun Mountain while descending into the St. Mary Valley, passing waterfalls, glaciers, and flower-adorned mountainsides. Explore St. Mary Lake in photo ops before stopping for an optional lunch or dinner at Rising Sun Motor Inn.

It is back for more on the return trip, leaving no doubt as to why this trip goes through what is called the Crown Jewel of the Continent.

Seldom seen by Glacier visitors is the Transportation Office, the hub of all tours in the park. When the snows begin to fall, the Reds go into hibernation here, parked snugly in the barns all winter, awaiting spring and another season in the park.

Buses meeting at Lunch Creek, the last section of
the Going-to-the-Sun Road to be completed.

A bus welcomes its guests with open doors.

As previous generations of buses pulls up to Lake McDonald Lodge, they remind visitors that not much has changed in the 80 years since these buses first became the primary means of transportation through Glacier National Park.

International Peace Park Tour

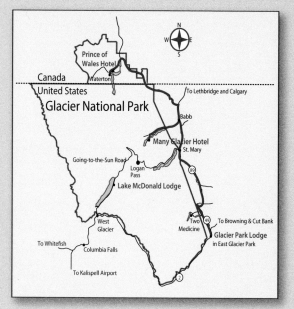

Travel the trails of the Blackfeet north on the Old North Trail, visiting arguably the most beautiful of all the Glacier Valleys: Swiftcurrent, and the famous Many Glacier Hotel. This is a perfect place to view three of the park's famous glaciers.

Then it is across the US/Canadian border (passport required) to the incredible Prince of Wales Hotel in Waterton Lakes Park. Stop there for lunch or tea, if you like, overlooking the Waterton town site and some of Glacier's highest peaks. This tour is the very best way to visit Chief Mountain and its many moods as it towers above the road most of the way.

Evening Wildlife Tour

John Muir called the Glacier scenery "care killing" and in the late afternoon, with the sun and shadows cascading over the mountains and valleys in an entirely different light, you will see the meaning of Muir's words. Travel Going-to-the-Sun Road to the top of the Continental Divide and St. Mary Valley as far as Jackson Glacier.

As the sun begins its slow descent behind Glacier National Park's Livingstone Range, it is an optimal time to view some of Glacier's most reclusive wildlife.

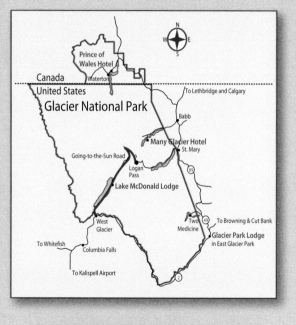

Visitors are reminded to always keep an eye out for some of Glacier's most famous inhabitants: bears, moose, bighorn sheep and the alpine-loving mountain goats.

Huckleberry Mountain Tour

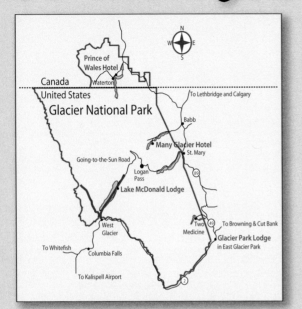

Immerse yourself in a Montana rain forest along the shores of Glacier's largest lake, Lake McDonald. Cedars, hemlocks, and tamaracks tower above you as you ride Going-to-the-Sun Road to the Avalanche Basin and the Trail of the Cedars. View Sperry Glacier, weather permitting.

Later, going up Camas Creek, it is a tale of three fires and forest rebirth. Enjoy good birding and wildlife viewing on the way to Huckleberry Mountain for a short stroll in a budding forest of lodge pole and tamarack. Wildflowers abound on this tour, along with great views into Glacier's illusive West Lakes District.

A National Historic Landmark, the Going-to-the-Sun Road was as much an engineering marvel when it was completed in 1933 as it is today. Engineers faced many challenges including, but certainly not limited to, how to build a road out of the side of a cliff. Thanks to their ingenuity, perseverance, and foresight, however, visitors to Glacier National Park have been rewarded with one of the most beautiful roads in America, if not the world, for the last 75 years. With a multiyear reconstruction project now in progress, visitors should be able to enjoy this marvel of engineering and beauty for another 75 years.

On the left is probably the most renowned structure on the road, the Triple Arches.

Once a Jammer Always a Jammer

They say Glacier National Park touches everyone who visits it. Majestic mountains etched forever into your memory, pristine forests whose tranquility calms all of your worries, and glacial waters so pure they cleanse your soul. Upon your first visit to this mountain paradise, you know you are home. A home not defined by walls and a roof, but by nature and peace, a home of the heart. A heart that, when not in Glacier, is always yearning to become whole again upon its next visit.

No group of individuals knows this better than the Jammers, the tour guides and drivers of Glacier National Park. For it is not only our pleasure to experience this park for a summer, it is our responsibility to share this Shangri-La with all who ride with us. To experience this park on a daily basis, to witness its ever-changing beauty, and to drive an exquisite 1930s bus over the most spectacular road, is both an honor and privilege. We get to live with the park, not in it or around it, but truly spend our summer as a part of this wondrous place.

What we are today is a direct result of who we have been over the past 95 years. Jammers have been a part of this park since 1914, and over the years, through various generations of both drivers and buses, we have developed a history rich in tradition, lore, and pride. Traditions that continue today as we drive the same buses over the same roads Jammers have since the beginning. And although the faces have changed, the Jammers are still here to inform and inspire all who visit Glacier National Park.

It is therefore my distinct honor and pleasure to thank all of the former Jammers for everything that we were, and for everything that has led us to where we are today. For everything that we are and for what we take pride in today, I would like to thank all of the current Jammers. And finally, for all of our potential and our continued attempt to be the best we can be, I would like to thank all of the future Jammers. Once Glacier gets into your blood, it never leaves; hence the saying, once a Jammer, always a Jammer.

We are the lucky ones.

David Eglsaer
Transportation Manager
Glacier Park, Inc.